Christine Pym

Little MOUSE'S BIG BREAKFAST

nosy crow

On a crisp cold day,
as the night crept in,
a hungry little mouse discovered
he had nothing to nibble for
breakfast the next morning.

He had searched every
sunflower for a seed
and every bush for a berry
but **all** the food had gone.
There was **nothing** to
be found at home.

Luckily, Little Mouse
knew **just** where to go.

He scampered along the path . . .

. . . up, up, up the drainpipe . . .

. . . until, finally,
Little Mouse . . .

. . . hopped through an open window.

And there, on the table, was a bright blueberry.

Well, Little Mouse **loved** a bright blueberry.

A bright blueberry would be just
perfect for a little mouse's breakfast.

Little Mouse was just about to go home
when he spotted something else . . .

. . . a rosy red apple.

Well, Little Mouse **loved** a rosy red apple!

A rosy red apple would be
delicious with a bright blueberry
for a little mouse's breakfast.

But then, behind
the rosy red apple,
Little Mouse
discovered . . .

. . . the big brown biscuits!

And, behind the big brown biscuits, he found . . .

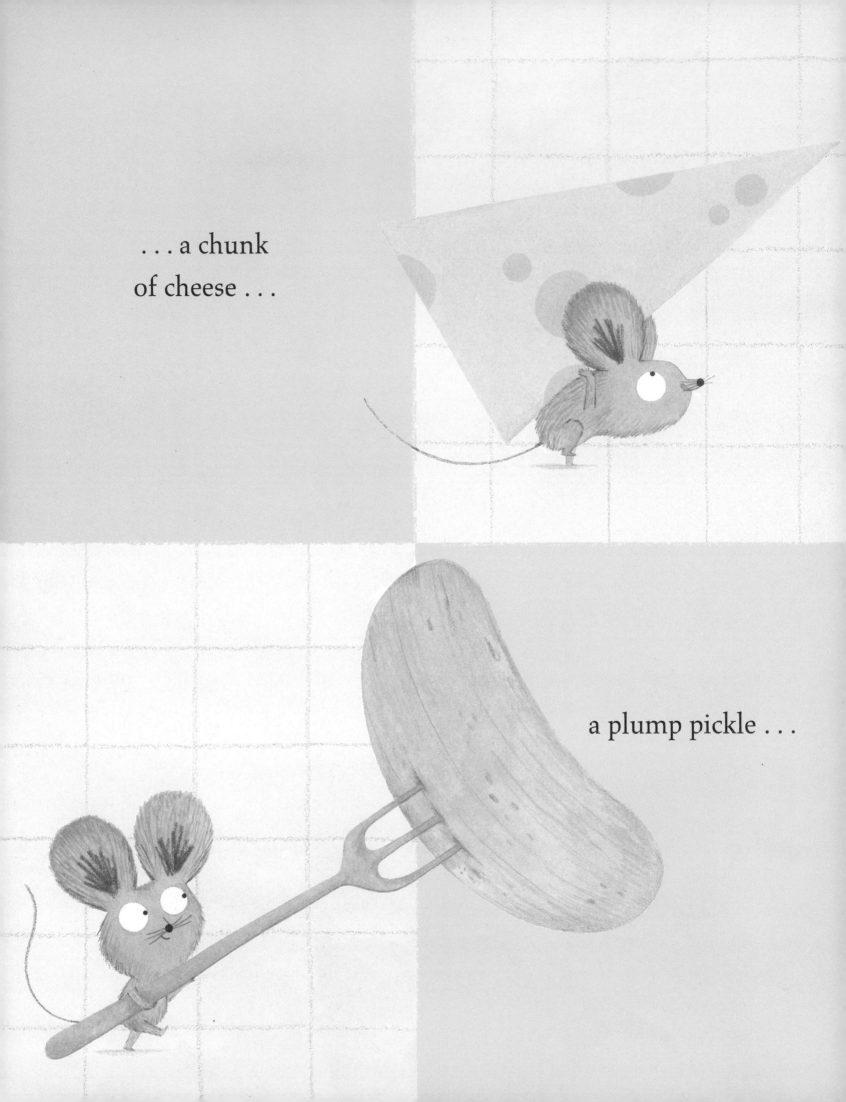

. . . a chunk
of cheese . . .

a plump pickle . . .

a spicy sausage . . .

. . . and a sweet,
sticky cupcake with
a cherry on top!

Little Mouse wasn't
sure if these things would
be **particularly** delicious,
but he decided to take
them anyway.

Little Mouse had
everything balanced . . .

. . . when he spotted
something special.

Something
very tasty . . .

. . . something he **knew** would
be just **perfect** for breakfast!

A shiny, stripy
sunflower seed!

What luck!

Little Mouse **loved** a
shiny, stripy sunflower seed!
A shiny, stripy sunflower seed
was his **favourite**.

But just as he reached out to pick it up . . .

. . . CRASH!

Little Mouse wasn't the only
one looking for breakfast.

The big black cat **loved** a little mouse!
A little mouse was his **favourite**.

A little mouse
would be just
perfect for
a big black
cat's breakfast!

Luckily, Little Mouse
knew **exactly** what to do.

He hopped out
of the window
and scampered . . .

. . . down,

down,

down

the

drainpipe . . .

. . . until, finally . . .

. . . Little Mouse
was home!

And so, on a crisp cold morning,
Little Mouse had his first
bite of breakfast.

It was perfect.
But it was small . . .
and it was getting smaller . . .

Little Mouse wasn't worried though.
He knew just where to go . . .

Next door!